WITHDRAWN

WITHDRAWN

The Real-Skin Rubber Monster Mask

Story by **Miriam Cohen**
Pictures by **Lillian Hoban**

Greenwillow Books New York

Watercolor paints were used for the full-color art.
The text type is Souvenir.

Text copyright © 1990 by Miriam Cohen
Illustrations copyright © 1990 by Lillian Hoban
All rights reserved. No part of this book
may be reproduced or utilized in any form
or by any means, electronic or mechanical,
including photocopying, recording, or by
any information storage and retrieval
system, without permission in writing
from the Publisher, Greenwillow Books,
a division of William Morrow & Company, Inc.,
105 Madison Avenue, New York, NY 10016.

Printed in Singapore by Tien Wah Press

First Edition 1 2 3 4 5 6 7 8 9 10

Library of Congress Cataloging-in-Publication Data
Cohen, Miriam.
The real-skin rubber monster mask / by Miriam Cohen;
pictures by Lillian Hoban.
p.   cm.
Summary: Second-grader Jim isn't sure what he wants to
be for Halloween but he knows he wants to be scary.
ISBN 0-688-09122-9. ISBN 0-688-09123-7 (lib. bdg.)
[1. Halloween—Fiction.   2. Fear—Fiction.]
I. Hoban, Lillian, ill.   II. Title.
PZ7.C6628Re   1990
[E]—dc20   89-34620   CIP   AC

*To the small person
who came to my door
in the real-skin
rubber monster mask*

Second Grade was in math groups, working on plusses.
George said, "For Halloween, I'm going to be a funny ghost."
"A ghost is boring! It's not even scary!" said Danny.
But Sara said, "That's only *your* opinion."

Jim said, "In First Grade, I always used to be funny at Halloween. But in Second Grade—I don't know why, I want to be horrible and disgusting."

"What are you going to be?" asked Paul.
"I didn't make up my mind yet," said Jim. Then he
began to worry. It was almost Halloween!

By the afternoon of Halloween, Jim
still couldn't decide what to be.

"You could be a clown," his mother said.
"A clown is *no* good! Anybody can be a little baby clown!"
said Jim. "In Second Grade you have
to be *really* scary."

So Jim and his mother went to the store to look at Halloween costumes. They looked at the witches, and Dracula, and a gorilla, and a robot. But Jim just couldn't decide.

Then Jim saw the Real-Skin Rubber Monster Mask,
Batteries Extra. It had flashing *eyes*, and green skin
dripping off its face, and a disgusting nose like a big gray wart.
"You wouldn't want *that,* would you?" asked his mother.
"Oh, yes, I would!" said Jim.

The minute they got home, Jim put on
the Monster Mask for his father.
"Yow! You scared me right into the
middle of next week," his father cried.

Jim ran to look in the bathroom mirror.
"This mask is *so great*," he said to himself.
"The kids are here!" called his mother.

The whole Second Grade was waiting on Jim's porch with their mothers or fathers.
Sammy was Dracula. George was a funny ghost.
Danny was a giant cockroach. Paul was Zorro.
Anna Maria was a princess *and* a bride.

Sara was She-Woman of the Universe.
And Willy was a meatball with spaghetti.
But he didn't get the meatball's eyes
in the right place, so Sammy had to take
his hand and show him where to go.

"What are you?" the kids asked Margaret.
"I'm a cinnamon doughnut," she said.
"You look like a bagel," Anna Maria told her.

"Jim, your mask is so neat!" everybody was saying.

"I know," said Jim. "I love it!"

"Let's go to the apartment house!" shouted Danny.

When they rang at Apartment 1A, the lady gave
them each a little package of candy corn.
"A monster! Isn't that nice!" she said to Jim.

"Come on," Danny called from the next apartment.
"They're giving good stuff in 1B! No raisins!"

When they left the apartment house, Jim
stopped to look in the big glass doors.
It was much darker than in his bathroom.
The monster's eyes looked so angry!
Jim could hear the green skin plopping off!
The gray wart nose looked as if it was
growing little, rotten, grabby fingers!

Suddenly Jim felt weird. Maybe the monster
was turning into him?
Or he was turning into the monster?
It was horrible! Jim pulled off his mask fast.

Paul said, "Why did you take your mask off,
Jim? It's *so neat!*"
"It's too hot," said Jim. He tried to leave the mask
under a bush, but Willy and Sammy said,
"Here, Jim! You almost lost your mask."

"Hah, hah! I knew it! Jim is scared of his own mask," said Danny.

But Paul said, "No, he isn't! Are you, Jim?"

"Of course not!" said Jim, but he did not put the mask back on.

"What's the matter with Jim?" asked Sara and Margaret.
"He's scared of that mask," said Anna Maria.
"He should have been a prince. Then he could have married me."

Paul said, "How could a person be scared of a mask when he bought it his own self?"

Willy and Sammy were whispering.
Then Willy said, "Hey, Jim!
How about if I'm the meatball
and you're the spaghetti?"

And Sammy started wrapping Willy's spaghetti around Jim.
"I'll carry your mask," he said, "and you can take
Willy around. Dracula doesn't look so cool with a meatball."

Jim and Willy almost beat Danny
onto Mr. Wiggins's porch.
Mr. Wiggins answered the bell.
"Would you look at this! Spaghetti,
a meatball, and a cockroach!
Did you ever see anything like it?"

And he gave them each a whole handful
of Little Ruthies, Caramel Sucker Pops,
and delicious pink bubble gum.

"Wow! Look how much I got!" Jim said to his mother.

When they got home and Jim was counting his candy,
he started chuckling to himself. "Next Halloween,
I'm going to be a funny clown. I just push a button
or something, and water squirts out of my ears!
People will be laughing and laughing."

And he jumped into bed with
his shopping bag next to him,
so he could feel it while
he was asleep.